This book belongs to

- -

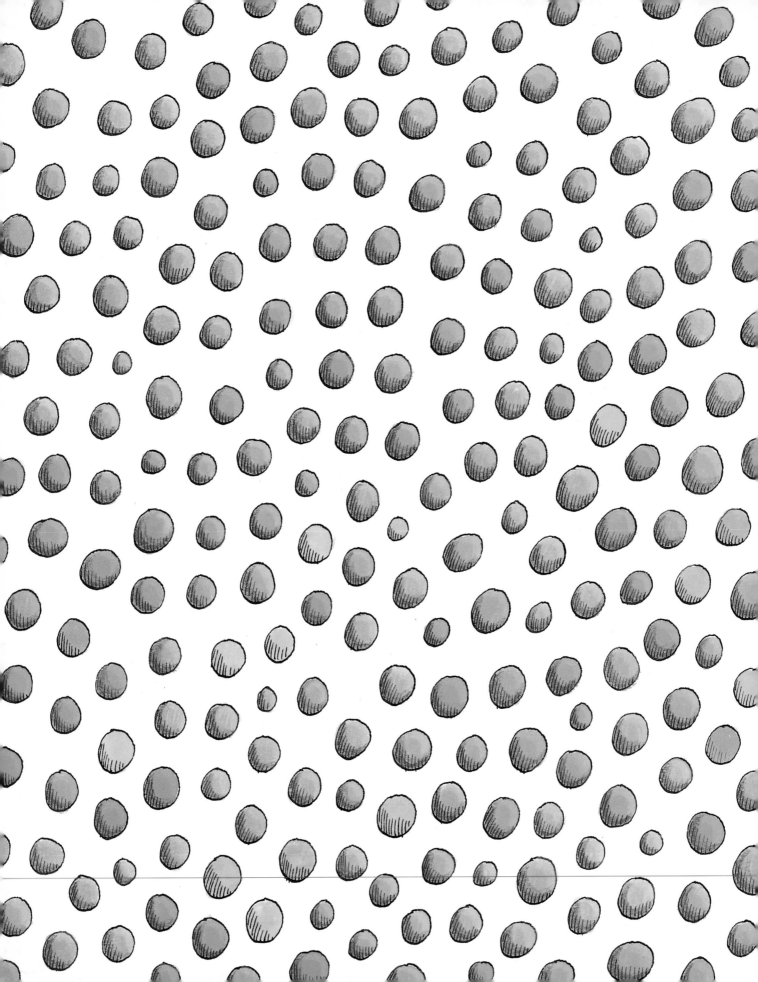

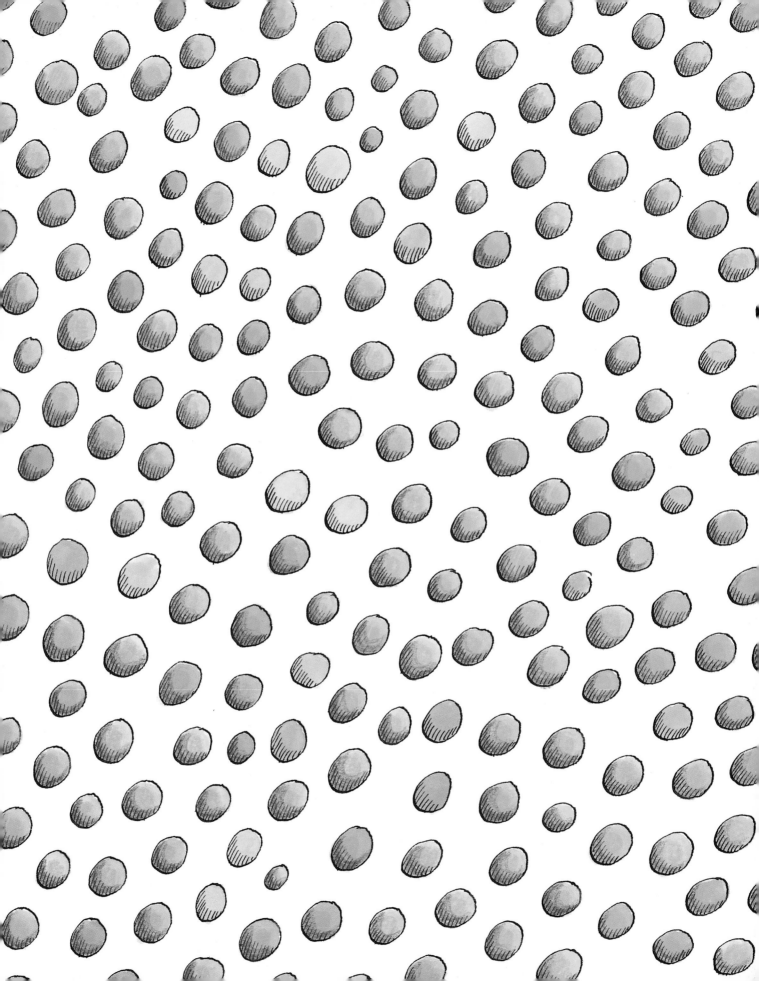

For Sam, Peb, Trish, and Ben.
With all my love, El.

tiger tales

an imprint of ME Media, LLC

202 Old Ridgefield Road, Wilton, CT 06897

Published in the United States 2005

Originally published in Great Britain 2005

By Scholastic Children's Books

A division of Scholastic Ltd

Text and illustrations copyright ©2005 Ella Burfoot

CIP data is available

ISBN 1-58925-395-7

Printed in Singapore

1 3 5 7 9 10 8 6 4 2

Louie
and the
Monsters

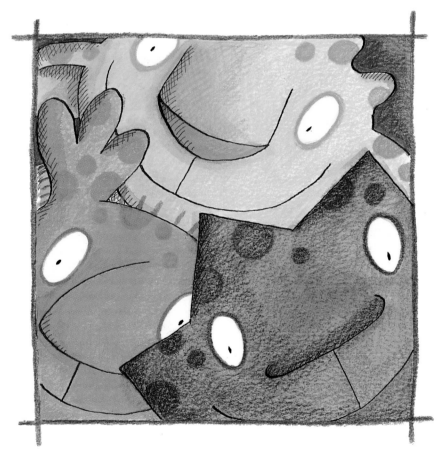

by Ella Burfoot

tiger tales

Louie didn't
like monsters,

but monsters
liked Louie.

They followed him
up the stairs . . .

**and all the way
back down again.**

They sat at the table and ate his dinner,
and got the peas stuck in their teeth.

They played silly games and broke
his toys, and they drew on the wall
with his favorite crayons.

They squeezed themselves into Louie's fort
until there was no room for him.

They dribbled and drooled . . .

and burped out loud!

Louie had had enough.
He shouted and screamed and jumped
up and down, and the monsters left the
house without a sound.

Then Louie climbed the stairs alone,

and ate his dinner on his own.

And he sat in his fort all by himself.
But the stairs were boring and he
hated peas ... and his fort was too big
with no one in it but him.

Monsters weren't really so bad.
Louie wished that he hadn't been
mean and shouted and screamed. He
wished most of all that the monsters
would come back.

He took some paper and his
favorite crayons and drew some
letters to make a word.

He took the word and a piece of tape,

and went and stuck it on the gate.

Then he went back to the house
and upstairs to his room.

su

Monsters liked Louie...

but Louie LOVED
monsters!

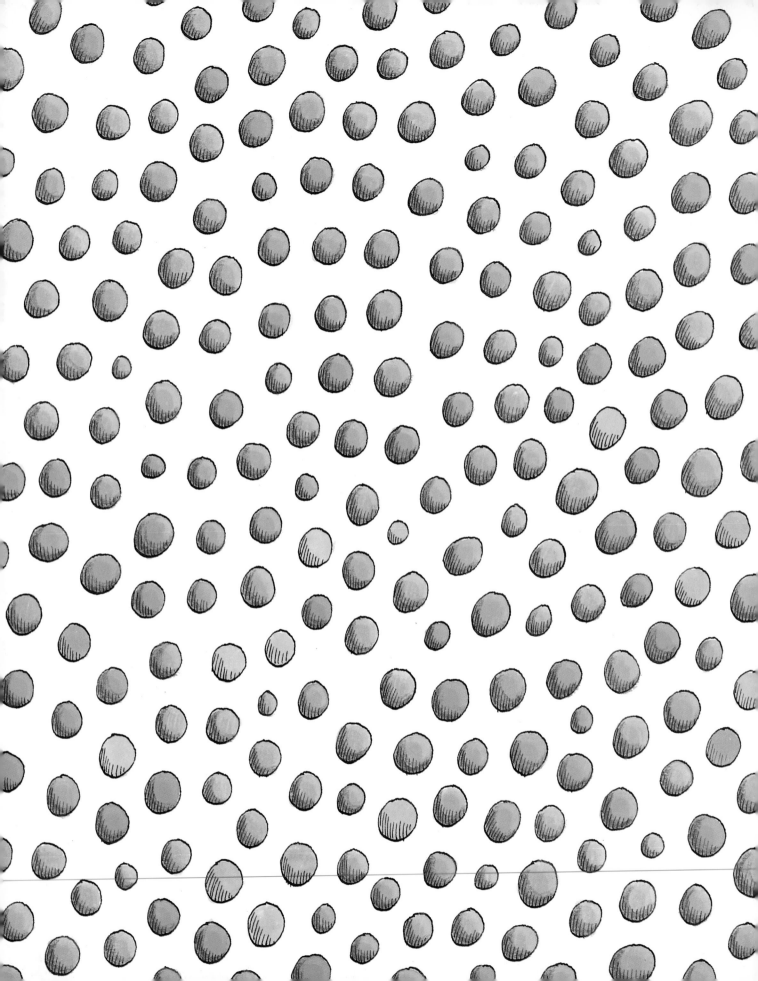